Roman Stories

Retold by Robert Hull
Illustrated by Tony Smith
and Claire Robinson

Wayland

Tales From Around The World

African Stories
British Stories
Egyptian Stories
Greek Stories
Native North American Stories
Norse Stories
Roman Stories

Editor: Katie Roden
Series Designer: Tracy Gross
Book Designer: Mark Whitchurch
Colour artwork by Tony Smith
Black and white artwork by Claire Robinson
Map on p. 47 by Peter Bull
Consultant: Dr Angus Bowie, The Queen's College, Oxford

First published in 1993 by
Wayland (Publishers) Ltd
61 Western Road, Hove
East Sussex BN3 1JD, England

Copyright © Wayland (Publishers) Ltd

British Library Cataloguing in Publication Data

Hull, Robert
Roman Stories.–(Tales from Around the World Series)
I. Title   II. Robinson, Claire
III. Smith, Tony   IV. Series
398.20937

ISBN 0-7502-0791-4

Typeset by Dorchester Typesetting Group Ltd
Printed in Italy by G. Canale & C.S.p.A., Turin
Bound in France by A.G.M.

Contents

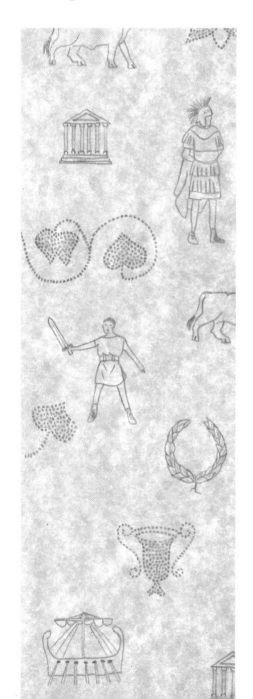

Introduction

When we say 'Londoners' we think of people living in London. When we say 'Romans' – 'ancient' Romans – we think of people living not just in Rome, but also in a hundred other cities spread across Europe, Africa and Asia, from Hadrian's Wall to the River Euphrates. That spreading around of Romans, which we now call the 'Roman Empire', happened over a long period of time.

At the beginning of the story of the Romans, before there even was a city called Rome, a small group of tribes lived in what is now central Italy. Gradually one tribe, the Latini, who lived near the River Tiber, became strong enough to build a town on the northern edge of their territory, Latium. That town was Rome, and it probably began life in the eighth century BC. The Latini grew stronger, the town became a city, the city a state, the state an empire.

The story of the founding of Rome is the famous tale of Romulus and Remus. Like any great people, the Romans had their own myths and legends, describing what happened in their far-distant past. But the Romans also enjoyed Greek myths and legends, and felt very close to the Greeks. Many of the myths and legends they told each other are the old Greek tales rewritten.

But liking Greek stories so much didn't prevent them from inventing their own. The Romans knew how to tell stories that 'grab' you. Many come from plays and long poems based on myths and legends. The most

4

famous Roman story is a long poem called *The Aeneid*. It has characters like those in Greek stories – but with Roman names, like Venus instead of Aphrodite. It is a marvellous, original story.

The Aeneid is the gripping tale of a few Trojans, led by Aeneas, escaping from Troy after it was burnt down, and wandering the Mediterranean for many years before settling in Italy. It is the story of the first 'Romans', a story of refugees driven from their homes by war, losing their families, but trying to survive. In one part there is one of the best, saddest love stories ever written.

The Romans particularly liked stories that were funny. This might be a bit surprising in a people who also liked roads and religion and governing others – serious things. But though they were serious people they also made fun of serious things.

Their gods, for instance. Greek gods were rather human. They had human feelings, and enjoyed life and its adventures; they were unreliable and interesting. When those gods became Roman some of them became a bit stiff and boring, like statues. That is perhaps one reason why Roman writers made such fun of them. When gods – or people – are too serious, we want to laugh. Readers of a famous book called *The Golden Ass* have laughed for centuries, especially at a story called 'Psyche and Cupid', which is one long leg-pull, mainly aimed at gods and goddesses.

You will have met Cupid. On 14 February you might have been sent a Valentine card – or two or three. It – they – may have had a drawing of a heart with an arrow through it. That was a Cupid's arrow, and the idea of Cupid and his arrows shot into people's hearts so they fall in love, comes from Roman stories.

A good story is like one of those arrows – it strikes you through, it roots you to the spot, keeps you in your seat, impales you.

Romulus and Remus

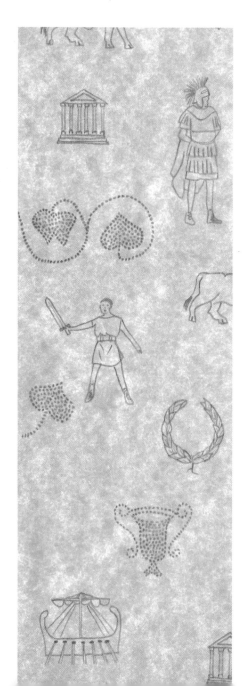

*A*mulius, king of Latium, the area of Italy that later contained Rome, won his throne by treachery. He banished the rightful king, his brother Numitor, and imprisoned Numitor's daughter to prevent her from having children. But she did have children: Romulus and Remus. The famous legend of Romulus and Remus describes how, as babies, they were thrown into the River Tiber, and suckled by a she-wolf.

Amulius looked down in hatred at the tiny shapes. They interfered with his plans. If he let them, they would ruin his future. How had it happened? Their mother had been shut away, and he'd done the hardest bit, getting rid of Numitor. He'd cleared a way to the throne, made certain of everything, and now these feeble things threatened to undo it all, to take his kingdom and land from him.

'Throw them in the Tiber.'

Amulius watched the two armed men go off down the track towards the river, the open crate swinging between them. He was going to make certain there was no last-minute hitch. He waited till he heard a splash, then turned back up the path to the city.

The night was warm and another storm threatened. The river was swollen from the day's downpours. The wolf paused.

She sniffed the air. Nothing. There had been nothing further downstream, either. The trail had gone. It had been here an hour ago, the two scents had been sharp in the grass and on the bank. They had played for a while here, while she left them for her food.

She saw the water was higher against the sand. She remembered a hollow in the bluff, a small cave, good to hide in. It had gone beneath somewhere. There was only the flood pouring past. The water had taken them.

By daylight the curve of the small beach ended in a sandy bank. The water had fallen by a foot or two, and well above the new water line were strewn bits of flotsam – broken branches, a corked jug, strands of weed and grass, a wooden crate.

She came down, sniffing amongst them, still hoping, weary. Flat scents of water, sand, leaf, wood; no sharp young body-scents, no hint of warmth or fur. Cold, empty air. On she went, to the end of the tiny beach. A warm shock came at her nostrils, then another. Not from the branches. Or the jug. From the wooden crate. She rooted forward amongst white things, wiggled her muzzle deep in them, and found breathing. Sleepy deep breathing.

She leapt back, snarling, puzzled. Then edged forward, nostrils working. It was young, something's young. There they were, with mud on them. They had flat, root-pale faces, with set-apart eyes. She sniffed near, licked the mud away from the face, and the eyes opened. It cried. The other gave a cry. Milk! Milk! it meant. She had that. Delicately she jumped her front paws over, straddled the crate and fed them.

They grew up wild, in a cave, without words. Instead of words, they learnt a thousand instructions of scent, sound and shape. They learnt weathers and seasons, love and loyalty, defending and killing.

Then they were stolen. A man saw them, a palace shepherd called Faustulus, and he picked them up from where they were playing, and ran home with them, one under each arm. The two boys were brought up as the shepherd's own sons. They learnt words, they learnt about plates and beds. It took a long time.

When they were older they became shepherds, helping their father guard the king's flocks. But though

7

they were shepherd's sons, they were still the once-fostered sons of a wolf. Their early education had been a training in wolf life. Their cub-memory lay across their human minds like a shadow.

They could be fierce easily. It showed when they helped the local shepherds, who were poor, and in winter often needed warm clothing and food. The brothers simply took them, by force, from the rich bandits who preyed on local people and passers-by. The brothers raided their hide-outs by night, working as silently and cunningly as the wolves they had watched and imitated.

There was something strange about those two, local people would say. About the way they walked together, looking round them, always on the alert. Or about the way they could be utterly still and composed, like statues. They seemed to understand each other without words.

Faustulus had never explained where they came from, until one day he was visiting an old neighbour of his. It was Numitor, once king of Latium, now a farmer, who had been living under armed guard ever since his brother, Amulius, stole the throne from him. Faustulus was trying to sympathize with Numitor and his sad life in exile, and told him the amazing story of his sons, who had lived in exile from human beings for the first few years of their lives.

He told Numitor how he had found two human boys near the Tiber, romping about with wolf cubs, and taken them home. They couldn't talk, had no clothes, and no idea what a chair was, or a house. It was amazing, unbelievable, but the truth was clear. They had spent those growing years as part of a wolf family.

Numitor had an immediate suspicion. Could they be the lost sons of his daughter Silvia? They were the right age. He must see them. Without revealing his suspicions, his hopes, he asked Faustulus to bring his sons to meet him.

A few days later, Numitor looked into the faces of the two young shepherds. His last doubts disappeared and he shook with joy. They had the looks, especially the eyes, of his daughter Silvia.

Numitor told them his story, how his brother Amulius had taken the throne from him, killed his two sons, sent Silvia to the temple of Mars as a kind of slave, and – as he and everyone else believed – had her sons drowned. Numitor told the brothers that he believed they were his two grandsons, the rightful heirs to the throne. At birth they had been called Romulus and Remus. Which, he wondered to them, was which?

The story made their eyes glint. They looked at each other for a while, not speaking. One touched the other's arm, looking hard at him. The other nodded. 'He is to be Remus, I Romulus. We have an important task to do now.' Abruptly, in silence, they left.

10

The news came to Numitor only a week later. Amulius had been killed in the night, and his body thrown into the Tiber. Who had killed him? No one seemed to know.

Then Romulus and Remus returned, and Numitor realized who had killed Amulius.

'A new king is needed for Latium!' cried Romulus.

'The old king!' shouted Remus.

And so Numitor became king again and returned to the palace he had been led from in chains twenty years before. His daughter Silvia was released from the temple that served as her prison, and saw her sons again.

In the joy of that reunion, the whole family – Numitor, Silvia, Romulus and Remus – went down to the Tiber to find the spot where the twins must have been found. They knew where Faustulus had seen them playing, but not where the wolf came upon the washed-up crate. The place they decided on, though, as if the gods were guiding them, was that same small, curving beach. They found a cave, which they called Lupercal, where they thought the wolf must have sheltered them.

The moment after they had decided on the place, they saw paw marks in the sand at the river's edge. They thought it was a good omen.

'The wolf-beings will protect us in their thoughts and doings. They are still here, and they remember us. They will continue to look after us.

'Once we lived as wolves and thought as wolves. We were wolves. We had no words to restrain us or help us understand. We had no tools, buildings, or gods. Let us build here, with words and tools, and make homes and temples.'

That night the howling of wolves was heard. It seemed another good omen. In the morning Romulus said, 'I have been given a name. In sleep the name of the city came to me. It was from my own name, as first of the twins, the older by a few minutes. The city is to be called "Rome", the city of Romulus.'

A shadow passed over Remus' mind. Remus had always been jealous of Romulus saying he was bigger, or stronger, or older. 'We must look for omens,' he said, 'to be certain.' Romulus agreed.

11

At dawn the next day the priest scrutinized the sky. There were six vultures in the part of sky the priest allotted to Remus, but twelve in the part given to Romulus. Romulus, he judged, was destined to be king.

Romulus began to plan his city. He ploughed a furrow where the walls were to be built.

Remus couldn't bear his brother behaving as if he were the only founder of the city. He laughed, running along the furrow, jumping over it and back again, mocking Romulus. 'Reme, not Rome!' he shouted. Romulus ran at him, screaming.

Remus felt a surge of fury. Quarrels of long ago came into his thoughts. They had often snarled and bitten at each other, and rolled on the ground in cub-like furies, but it had never been serious. They had never hurt each other.

But here was a fight much more serious than those of long ago. There was no play or pretence in it. They were fighting over what name to give the city, and who should be king. Even though they were brothers, even though Numitor tried to restrain them, saying it didn't matter, they could share the throne and call the city by different names, or both names.

No. They both wanted the same thing, and the shadow of their old wolf-being told them that being brothers did not count any more. They were no one's sons, they were enemies. That other creature wanted all the land, all the food, air and sunlight for himself. That other must go, even if it had been called 'brother'. Must go, or be taken away, or die.

'The land is mine,' Romulus thought, 'the city must bear my name.'

'The land is mine,' Remus thought, 'the city must bear my name.'

Inside their heads they could hear no other words but 'my city, my city'. Their wolfish greed returned to them, even though they had been learning to be human.

In the fight it was Remus who died.

So there was a city called Rome.

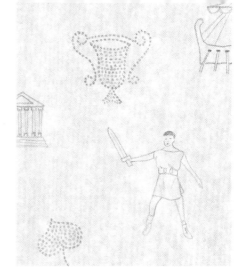

Pure Magic

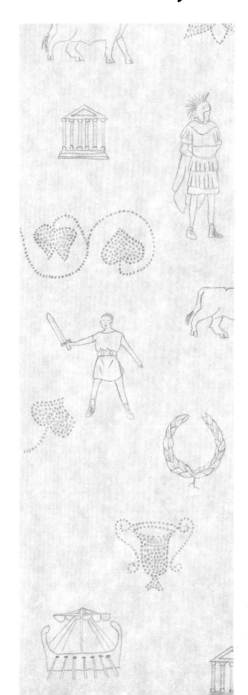

$\mathcal{L}$ucius, a merchant from Carthage, in Africa, was resting in the shade of a fig tree at the side of a dusty road just outside the town of Hypata, in Thessaly. He had come there to sell his jewellery, but also because he had heard that Hypata was a famous centre of sorcery, and Lucius, more than anything, wanted to learn about magic. It was his passion in life.

He was roused by voices. Two men had stopped by the tree to continue an argument.

'That's a ridiculous story! Innkeepers turning guests into frogs, a house that sings! Pigs with wings! I don't believe a word!'

'Magicians can do anything. They can turn the moon to green cheese.'

'Nonsense!'

'They can make rivers run backwards and stop waterfalls and make the stars sail round in circles.'

'That's rubbish, rubbish! Anyway, stars do go round in circles.'

'They don't.'

'They certainly do. There's nothing magic about that, or about the other things. They can be explained naturally.'

Now Lucius loved any kind of argument about magic. He scrambled to his feet. 'Can I walk along with you and join in your fascinating talk? I am interested in magic. In fact I have come to Hypata from Carthage, to learn magic.'

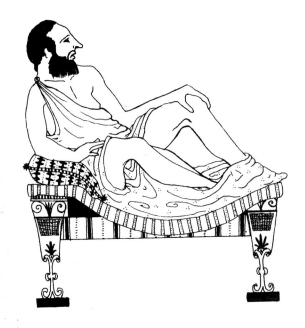

'You've come from Carthage to Hypata to learn magic?' said the doubting one.

'Yes,' said Lucius proudly.

'Well, there's a miracle for you. Anyway, join us and try to make me believe in my friend's unbelievable stories.'

So Lucius went along with the two men, who carried on arguing about whether horses can be taught geometry or monkeys ever rob banks, and other interesting matters. Then they mentioned some well-known local wizards and witches, and Lucius was especially interested to hear that in Hypata lived a famous sorceress called Pamphile, wife of Milo the Meany.

'That's his house, there, why don't you call on them?'

Here was Lucius' opportunity. He had come all the way from Africa for this. 'I think I will,' he said. 'Goodbye and thank you for your interesting company.'

Lucius was very nervous. He was outside a famous house of magic in the capital city of magic. He trembled as he knocked on the door. A beautiful servant girl opened it.

'Yes?'

He was so overwhelmed he could hardly speak.

'Er . . . rr, I would like to meet Pam-pam-ph-phile the Sor-cor-cer-eress,' he said.

'Who the what?' the girl said.

He tried again, slowly. 'Pam-phil-e, the fa-famous sor-cer-ess.'

'Ah . . . yes. No. Not unless you have lots of spare cash with you.'

'I am prepared to pay well. To learn sorcery. I'm hoping to set up a magic business in Carthage. At the moment I am a jeweller.'

'Come in then, what are you hanging about on the mat for?'

Lucius was taken into a dining-room. A thin man in torn, dirty clothes was lying on a sagging, threadbare couch. Was that Milo?

It was. 'Come in,' he said. 'My name is Milo. Here is my wife.' His wife – Pamphile the famous sorceress –

was sitting on the floor. Perhaps it was for magic reasons. She gave Lucius half a smile.

'Do sit down,' Milo said, 'and have some lunch.' Lucius stared at 'lunch', on a plate on a small table next to the couch. There were two figs and a six-inch length of yellow fish. 'There's enough for two.'

Pamphile left – it seemed there wasn't enough food or furniture for three. 'Take Pamphile's place. Excuse the shortage of chairs and furniture. We sold them as a precaution against burglars. So, you'd like to study my wife's skills?'

Lucius said he would, and it was soon agreed that he should stay for a while in Milo's house. At a fee. Plus rent. Two months in advance. Food not included. No money back if not satisfied. Some jewellery would suffice for a deposit.

Lucius agreed to it all. He was very keen to learn magic.

Milo called the servant girl. 'Fotis, take Lucius to the spare room, and then to the public baths – the water in the house isn't hot enough.'

On the way to the baths, in answer to Lucius' questions, Fotis told him about Milo and Pamphile, about what a monster miser he was, and how Pamphile used her sorcering tricks mainly to make men love her because Milo was so mean to her.

On the way back from the baths she told him more secrets. She described how Pamphile was trying to make a handsome blond called Leontas fall in love with her.

'How does she do it?' asked Lucius, eager to start his education.

'Well, she's trying out a new method. On the day Leontas goes to the hairdresser's, she's going to send me to get some of his cut-off hair. The plan is, I buy something for Pamphile and while the hairdresser's wrapping it up in the back of the shop, I whisk bits of Leontas' blond hair off the floor and take them to Pamphile.'

Lucius stopped to write it all down in his little notebook. But he was baffled. 'Then what?'

'I think Pamphile does a charm to make the owner of the hair come to get it back. At night. You throw the

hair on a fire and the pain and smell make them come running. Something like that.'

By now they were back at Milo's house, and Lucius rushed inside to write down the rest of this interesting information before he forgot it.

The next day, as it happened, was an important day in Hypata. It was the first day of Laugh Week. Pamphile had found out that Leontas had made an appointment for a haircut that afternoon, so she sent Fotis off on her errand. Before she went, Fotis invited Lucius out – 'for some laughs,' she said – to the house of a friend of hers that evening, after she came back from her errand.

She arrived at the hairdresser's just at the right time, as he was dusting the hair off Leontas' shoulders. When Leontas had gone she asked for a box of the hair gel that Pamphile used. While the hairdresser was in the back of the shop she scooped up several lengths of curly, yellow hair and stuffed them down her blouse.

Then the plan went wrong. The hairdresser, unfortunately, saw Fotis as he came back, and told her to give him his hair back. Off home she had to go, without any of Leontas' hair.

Within a few seconds Fotis was sent an inspiration. Just round the corner was a butcher's shop, and hanging on hooks outside were three goatskins, tied at the neck and blown up, waiting to be filled with wine. The butcher had just given the skins a final trim, ready for taking them round to the wine merchant down the street, and Fotis was quick to see that some of the goat's hair that had been cut off and fallen on the pavement was a similar colour to Leontas' blond crop. She grabbed some. Pamphile wouldn't notice the difference.

And she didn't. When Fotis came back Pamphile went straight off to the top of the house to start her magic with the goat's hair, thinking it was her beloved's offcuts. Meanwhile Fotis and Lucius left for their party, late in the afternoon, intending to have a comical evening. Lucius thought he might also pick up some more magic ideas.

For the next few hours, in her magic workshop at the top of the house, Pamphile worked lovingly on the

17

goat's hair. She wondered about the strange, rather strong smell it had, but decided it must be some perfume the hairdresser used.

She plaited the hair, bathed it in essence of roses, kissed it seven times, and sang seven magic love songs to the stars. Then she lit a stick of incense, made a pyre of seven love poems and sang to the goddess of love, Venus. This was the climax of the magic. 'Come, soul of love, come, handsome owner of beautiful hair, come to me, knock at the door of my loving house.'

Which is just what happened. The magic started to operate. The goatskins, filled with wine now, squatting on the pavement outside the wine shop, unhooked themselves from the wine merchant's wall, and went bumping and squelching up the street. Three or four people who'd come round the corner, walking home late from a party, paused for a moment, then turned and ran.

Soon the bounding wineskins arrived at Milo's gate, and started swinging and bumping themselves at it. Pamphile's magic had worked. Her lovers had arrived.

Meanwhile, Lucius had been having a very entertaining evening at Fotis' friend's house. He'd laughed a lot, eaten a lot, and drunk a lot. Now he walked along in the moonlight, staggering out of one street and into another, on his way back.

He had heard some scary magic stories that evening, too, about people being turned into lamps and mice and stones. When a cat slunk across in front of him he shuddered. Perhaps it was a witch on her rounds. He'd also heard that there were robbers on the street late at night. He took his sword out and peered ahead into the shadows.

The last corner. This was the street. That was the door – but what were those dark shapes clustered round it, heaving themselves against it, trying to break it down? Fat robbers in big, dark cloaks! Full of drink and dare-doing! Lucius was full of drink and dare-doing too, so he charged amongst them, hacking and slashing with his sword. They would run away! No, they didn't, they stood their ground. But Lucius, what bravery, what swordsmanship! One wheezed and sank to his knees, another gasped and wobbled, the third sighed and keeled over. In no time three soggy shapes lay crumpled at his feet, red blood flowing dark in the moonlight. Being a hero was magical!

It was late. Lucius decided not to wake anyone, but to go straight to bed, leaving the bodies to be cleared away the following day. Next morning, when he went down to receive the thanks of Milo and Pamphile, and of course Fotis, instead of being praised for his brave burglar-slaughtering, he was arrested. A sergeant and constable said that they had reason to believe that Lucius was responsible for the three innocent corpses found outside Milo's front door. They charged him – in the local Thessalian dialect, which he didn't understand – with 'multiple skinicide' and 'grievous baggily harm' and one or two other things, and took him off to the court. The officers were grinning, which he didn't understand either, and thought was a bit unfair.

All of Hypata seemed to know about the trial. Those who weren't gaping and grinning down in the road leaned out of windows or hung onto statues or squeezed in at the courtroom windows and up to the

20

rafters. There were curious smirks everywhere.

Lucius thought he was doomed, but he spoke up for himself, describing how the captain of the burglar band came at him in the dark with a fierce cry of 'At 'im lads!' and explaining how, even when they surrounded him with their swords drawn, he managed to fight them off. 'It was all done in self-defence,' he said.

There were giggles in court. Lucius couldn't understand. It seemed serious to him.

The judge stood up. 'Ahem. Silence in court while the judge blows his . . . I shall now pronounce a sentence. This murderer here, the murderer of three innocent . . .' he paused, 'of three innocents who had barely set foot on life's path, must be punished. And so that he understands the gravity of his crime, he must look again on the savaged, severed, gory, gruesome, lifeless,' – here the judge had to stop to blow his nose, and everyone in court giggled and snorted again – 'pathetic forms that he so murderously, mindlessly and . . . er . . . mercilessly . . . er . . .'

'Mauled!' someone shouted.

'Mangled!' came from someone else.

'Mauled, yes, and mangled. Open the coffins!'

A sergeant hauled Lucius across the floor of the court to the coffins. He pushed Lucius forward. Another sergeant, his hand over his face, took off the coffin lids.

There was a sudden silence in court. Lucius looked into the coffins, stared for a few seconds, bent down and reached his hand into one, then stood up and looked round the court, bewildered. He had seen three . . . surely, they were . . .

There was a din of laughter. People were collapsing on each other's shoulders. The two sergeants were hugging each other and shaking with laughter. The judge was mopping his streaming eyes with his handkerchief. Fotis was smiling.

In Hypata, on Day Two of Laugh Week, for a practical joke, they always arranged a mock trial. Lucius wasn't to know that, but now, as he looked round, he was beginning to find out. And he later realized that for the people of Hypata, his trial was pure magic.

Cupid and Psyche

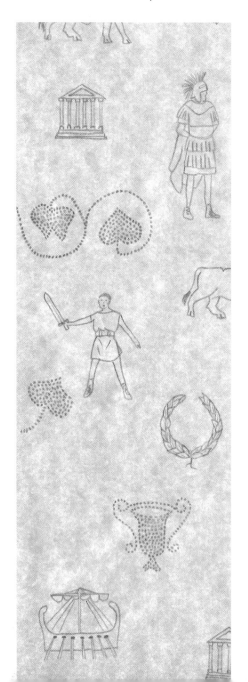

*O*nce there was a young woman who was very beautiful. She was the daughter of the local king and queen, and she had two older, fairly horrid sisters, who weren't a bit beautiful. This young woman, Psyche, was so beautiful that people stopped her in the street and said, 'My, aren't you gorgeous?' and things like that.

Venus, the goddess of love, went dotty with jealousy. She herself, Venus the Devastating, was supposed to be the most beautiful creature there ever was, will be or had been, and she objected to the fuss people were making over a girl who was only human, not even a goddess.

Well, Venus, the old crosspatch – actually, she's forever young, so I should say Venus, the forever young crosspatch – decided to take it out on Psyche, to get revenge on her for being so beautiful. Which sounds silly, doesn't it, but that's goddesses for you.

Anyway, people treated Psyche as if she were Venus herself, and finally Venus couldn't stand it anymore. She said to her son, Cupid – the one with the love-arrows – she said to him, 'I want you to do a little job for me. There's a girl called Psyche. She needs stopping. People, stupid people with no eyes in their heads, think she's as beautiful as me. Just fancy that! The silly creature goes strolling about drinking it all in, thinking she's just marvellous and the best thing since sliced figs. I want you to teach her a lesson. I want you to make sure she falls in love with someone ghastly –

or even better some*thing* ghastly. At once, if you don't mind. So, just you fly off and do a proper son's duty for your gorgeous mother. I haven't asked for anything like this for a long time.'

Cupid had a long list of other things to do, including several love affairs to start with a batch of sharp new arrows, but off he went anyway. Mother Venus flying round in a bad mood wasn't worth sharing the sky with.

Meanwhile Psyche's mother and father were worried that she still wasn't married. Her older sisters had been married to local kings years before, one to a miserable, bald bore older than her father, the other to a sciatical little skinflint. Why the king and queen wanted Psyche to follow her sisters up to the altar only they could tell. But they did. In fact, they were so anxious for her to marry that finally they went for advice to the temple of Apollo.

The priest on duty sang a few lines of poetry which said that Psyche had to get married on a certain mountain the week after next. That part was all right, but when the priest went on to say that the husband would be a 'winged pest', and a 'nuisance', it didn't sound encouraging at all.

They wished they hadn't been to the priest, if the answer was that Psyche had to marry some sort of monster. Still, a god's prophecy has to come true, and you might as well help it to. In fact a prophecy's as good as an order, so Psyche and her parents came back fourteen days later with Psyche dressed up for the marriage ceremony.

It was a real funeral of a wedding. Psyche's mother and father were in tears and everyone looked grim and disappointed. The prophet had said that Psyche must be left on the mountain, and when she was alone her husband would come to her. So after they had said their goodbyes, off everyone went, leaving Psyche alone. A real cheery moment. It didn't seem right, they all said.

Now the next part of the story is very strange. Psyche was standing on the hilltop, watching them all disappear down the mountain, when she felt a sudden breeze spring up. Then her clothing was disturbed by a

23

surging warm wind that came up the mountainside and flowed all round her. It blew stronger and stronger, till she felt herself being lifted into the air, as if she were in a dream. She was carried over trees, then high above a river, then down into a small clearing by a forest stream. There she lay down exhausted and fell asleep.

When she woke it was late in the afternoon, and she started walking. Soon she saw a glimmer of light through the trees. She walked and walked, nearer and nearer, until she came to – of course – a palace! She wandered in; there were silver walls, bronze doors waiting open, and inside even more amazing things – all the millionaire trimmings – mosaic floors, gold statues, mirrors on the ceiling, thick carpets on the sweeping staircase.

Then Psyche heard a voice, 'Well, do you like it? This palace is yours, all yours. This is your personal maid speaking. Here is your new home, specially decorated and furnished exclusively for you. Take the first left for the bathroom. Your invisible attendants will wait on you there.'

And they did. She saw no one, but everything was done for her. Voices without bodies spoke to her. Invisible hands poured water and brought towels. The same with supper: voices asked her what she wanted; invisible hands served food, poured wine, cleared the table and played beautifully on the lyre.

I wonder if you can guess what happened next? Psyche still hadn't seen her new husband, but when she went to bed and blew out the candle he visited her. Unfortunately, like everyone else in this strange palace he wasn't visible. Perhaps he was ugly, a genuine monster. She was madly curious, but he seemed to love her. He said he did, anyway, though he left her before daylight.

The same thing happened the next time he came to visit her, and the next. He even made her promise that she wouldn't try to see him. He said she could live in the palace and love him each night as long as she didn't look at him or want him to stay through the day.

At first Psyche enjoyed her married life. She disliked not seeing her husband, and she saw no one else, but he came with his love each night, there were voices to talk to, and she had everything else she needed. But she began to be restless. She wasn't really happy, and wouldn't be until she knew who her husband was. Also, she wanted to see her family, especially her two sisters, to get their advice.

'Lovely, nameless husband with no face,' she said one night, 'I long to see you, but if that is not permitted, at least let me see my two sisters. Let them come for a good sister-to-sister talk and tell me about my family.'

Now Cupid – you've realized who she was married to, of course, haven't you? – Cupid didn't want her sisters to come and get suspicious about the whole arrangement, but he felt sorry for Psyche, and so he agreed. The one condition was that Psyche wasn't to say anything at all about her husband – who he was, what he looked like, or anything. Psyche agreed. She was overjoyed: 'Ah, husband, thank you. You are so kind to me. I couldn't love you more if I could see you, and you were Cupid himself.'

The next day the sisters went to the mountaintop, waiting for a surge of magic wind to deliver them to Psyche's palace. Down they were soon wafted, not knowing they were allowed to travel on the winds of love only by special permission of their brother-in-law Cupid. The laws of love were only in operation in those parts when he was visiting.

The sisters gazed in amazement at the sumptuous furnishings of the palace, then their faces froze in alarm as they were served wine by the invisible servants. But, though they were quite scared, they still asked a hundred questions a minute, and though they were madly curious, they were even more insanely jealous. Such luxury, such wealth! What luck! How unfair! It nearly made them sick on the spot.

When they asked her about her husband, Psyche made up a tale about a handsome young husband who was a famous hunter and often away all day. At the end of the visit she gave the sisters presents of some very expensive jewellery, and off they went, borrowing the ever-ready winds of love.

What mutterings and sneerings the sisters enjoyed on their way home! 'Did you see that kitchen floor? Gems and rubies in a kitchen! How vulgar! And all those invisible servants! But she does have a rich, handsome husband, not one like mine, stony broke and bald as a melon.'

'And did you see her clothes? Hundreds of dresses with gold thread, and rows and rows of shoes and cloaks! I don't get a thousandth of what she gets for clothes. Fancy me being married to a miserly mini-person! I really can't stand him, the creaky old conker-bonce! I hate her too, the snooty snob, showing off like that, ordering the winds about and getting us blown off the premises as soon as she feels like it.'

The two sisters were quite carried away with fury and self-pity. They were determined to spoil their sister's happiness if they could. But how?

Meanwhile Cupid realized that the sisters would soon be up to some nasty trick. He warned Psyche. He told her to beware of their scheming, and never to say anything about him, especially that she couldn't see him when he visited her.

The sour sisters called a second time a few days later. They hadn't been invited, but the wizardly winds carried them just the same.

They were cunning. They asked some of the same questions again, to see if Psyche had been telling the truth about her husband the first time. Psyche wasn't prepared for this. She forgot what she had invented before, and this time made up a different story, about a rich, handsome, middle-aged merchant who was always travelling abroad. At the end of the visit, away the sisters came with even more jewellery, seething with even more jealousy.

'So,' the younger one sneered as soon as they were out of sight, 'So our dear sister doesn't know who she's married to! That means he's invisible. A god! The cunning little schemer! Landed a god! What on earth shall we do . . . ?' The two of them spent a terrible night wondering how they could stop Psyche being lucky and happy. Neither of them slept half a wink.

Next morning the older sister had a horribly clever inspiration. 'I know what we'll do . . . Listen. Remember the priest's prophecy, about her marrying something monstrous? Well, we tell her that she's married to the front end of a mile-long snake that whispers love at night and slides into its cave in the daytime. She'll have to look at it just to check, and then her lovely husband will disappear from her life for ever. Ha! That'll sort her.'

'Brilliant,' the other said. 'Let's rush down to her palace again.'

In a few minutes, by the usual magic mountain wind, they were at the palace, saying that they'd come in a hurry to tell her some important news.

27

'What news?' Psyche said. 'You were here only a couple of days ago. Why didn't you tell me then? My husband will think you're up to something.'

'Up to something? Us? Your loving sisters?' one of the sisters said, 'Psyche, how could you? But anyway, you'd better have our news. It's not good news, we're afraid.'

'No, it isn't,' the other said.

'Well?'

'Your husband's a snake. We thought you ought to know. We know you don't know. We know you can't see him for what he is. Next time he calls we suggest you light a candle and take a quick glance. It's the only way you'll find out who you're married to, to examine him in the light. We're terribly sorry for you. We're only thinking of your happiness, and can't bear to think of you married to a snake, even if he's quite a loving snake.'

Psyche screamed at them. 'Get out! Get out of my husband's palace this instant!'

But the sisters hadn't finished. 'What we suggest is that you have a knife ready when you take a look at your snake of a husband. You can kill the snake with your knife, then afterwards you can have all his treasure, marry someone visible, and live happily and wealthily ever after.' Then they left, saying how sorry they were, grinning and smirking at each other.

Psyche thought and thought about what her sisters had said. She knew they were wrong. She could see they were crazed with jealousy, and capable of inventing anything to hurt her.

They were lying. Her husband couldn't possibly be a snake. Yet she still didn't know why she couldn't see him, or why he never stayed with her in the day. Perhaps there was something awful about him, something so strange it couldn't be imagined.

28

Over the weeks Psyche fought down her curiosity, but one night it overwhelmed her. Her husband was asleep. She slipped out of bed and tip-toed to the table in the next room where she left the candle each night. With her heart beating hard she came near to the bed, and brought the lamp close to her husband's sleeping face.

Cupid! The god of love himself was her invisible husband! Everything became clear – her sisters' envy, her husband's behaviour, the prophecy, the anger of Venus behind it all. She stood looking at him, the shadows from the candle wavering across his face. She was trembling. Beads of hot wax ran down the shaking candle. Two or three fell from it onto Cupid's tender white shoulder. Suddenly he was awake, staring into her eyes!

Alert in a moment – the gods wake quickly – Cupid spoke. 'I asked you not to try to find out who I was. Now it is over. You have ruined it. I cannot come here again. I am a god. Venus, my mother, ordered me to make you fall in love with someone worthless, or worse. Instead I fell in love with you myself, knowing that we could only be together in the strange way we have been. I have never been able to make myself visible to you, and never been able to stay with you. It was better than not having your love at all, and perhaps for you it was better than never loving me. Now I must leave you. Also my shoulder hurts.'

And without a sound Cupid went from the room and drifted up on slow, white wings into the dark sky. She had lost him.

For the next few days, Psyche was too grief-stricken to do anything. She just wept, brooded and despaired. Then, with some energy coming back to her, she set out to find her husband. For weeks she went from city to city, asking people if they had seen him. Once, on a country road, she met the god Pan, who advised her to seek help from – guess who? – Cupid, god of love. So much for the wisdom of the gods.

After a while, Psyche arrived in the city where her eldest sister was queen, and went to see whether she had any news. Her sister went dizzy with jealousy all over again, this time at the thought that Psyche had

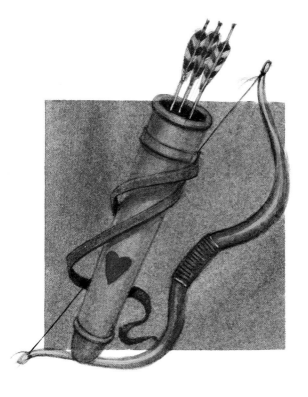

29

been loved by Cupid, and she decided she would be his wife instead. Telling her husband that her old mother had died, she immediately set off for the mountain. She launched herself from the cliff into the wind, as she had done before, calling out, 'Here comes a woman truly worthy of your love, Oh Cupid.' Unfortunately the wind didn't work, because now that Cupid was elsewhere his magic powers were off duty, and she plunged to her death on the rocks below. Later, exactly the same thing happened to the other sister, when Psyche went to see her.

Psyche decided to ask for help from the gods. She went to a temple, and prayed to Juno. Juno wouldn't help; she was scared of the young god of love, Cupid, fearing the damage he could do with his arrows. She was also wary of his mother, Venus. From the gossip going round the gods, Juno knew that Venus had found out about Cupid's escapade, and was furious that he had disobeyed her orders. What made it worse was the rumour – it was true – that Psyche was going to have Cupid's child.

Venus in her fury spent a few days rampaging round hunting for Psyche, but she was too lazy and snooty to keep on looking hard herself. Instead she sent Mercury, the errand-god, to do her searching for her. But by that time Psyche had decided to go to Venus anyway. Venus was her mother-in-law, after all, and might know where Cupid was. Soon enough the two met. Psyche arrived at the palace one afternoon while Venus was having a rest.

A servant announced her. 'A young woman, a certain Psyche, has come to see you, goddess.' In a few moments Venus came from her bedroom, looking sleepy and beautiful, her robe trailing on the marble floor. In a fraction of a second, realizing who Psyche was, her face changed from sleepy and lovely to awake and evil. She went wild. She flew at Psyche with her beautiful long red nails and tore at her hair, swearing and fuming and accusing her of luring her son into a hopeless marriage by disgusting trickery. Then she calmed down and wept.

After a while she stopped and looked hard at Psyche. 'You are going to be a mother soon. I hate the idea of you having my son's child, and I don't intend to be a granny yet anyway. I will allow the marriage only if you can prove to me that you *are* the daughter of a king and queen, and not what I think you are, a common servant girl.

'To prove that you are worthy of Cupid, you must go to Tartarus, the kingdom of death, and visit the beautiful Queen Proserpine. Take this box. I want a milligram or two of her beauty. I've run short recently, because I haven't had the time to repair my appearance. What with all this running about and tension, I don't look as well as I should, and I have a divine dinner party coming up next week.'

Psyche sensed that she was being sent along the road to her death. But even if she could not refuse the journey, she could at least refuse the route Venus gave her. She would find her own way to die.

She started out from Venus' palace. There was a stone tower at the roadside, tall enough to throw herself from. She climbed to the top, and was just about to jump when she heard a voice coming from the stone. 'No, no, Psyche, no. Live, live. Listen to me. You can go to Tartarus to see Proserpine and fill the box with her beauty. It is possible. Listen to my instructions.'

The tower told her exactly which way to go, and what to do and not do. She had to take two coins to pay Charon, the ferryman, who would then carry her over the River Styx and back again later. To quieten Cerberus, the fearsome guard-dog, she needed two drugged bones, one for each journey. The final instruction was, on no account to open the box that Proserpine would give her, filled with her beauty.

Following the instructions of the tower's stony voice, Psyche accomplished the dangerous journey to Tartarus. Charon agreed to ferry her over the Styx, and Cerberus took the bone, slumped in a drugged sleep and let her pass. She met Proserpine, and had the box filled. She made her way back to the upper world, and came out into the light. Never had the sky seemed so beautiful. She was so overwhelmed with joy that she sat down by a stream. She was safe! Soon she would see Cupid. Then she thought how awful she must look

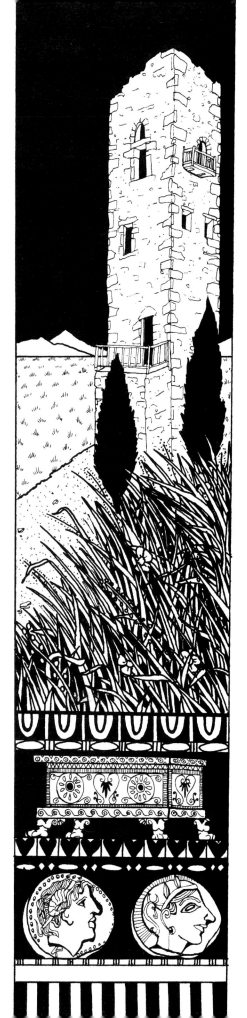

after the long, exhausting journey through the smoky underworld.

She must look her best for Cupid. Perhaps . . . perhaps if she used the tiniest fleck, no more than an eyelash's weight, of what was in the box . . . She prised the lid open a fraction, and immediately fell into a deep sleep. All that there was in the box was the sleep of death.

It was lucky for Psyche that she was so exhausted that she fell asleep at the first whiff of death from the box. If she had opened the box properly, it would have been the end of the story, and Venus would have had her revenge.

Meanwhile, Cupid's mother was trying to keep him indoors, 'till the scar from his burn heals,' she said. (Fancy pretending a few hot drops of candlewax could leave a scar!) But Cupid escaped and fled to Jupiter. He told the greatest of the gods the whole story, saying how much he loved the mortal Psyche.

Like most of the gods, Jupiter had seen what was going on, and thought that Venus had been behaving in a very mean, un-godlike way. He had hoped she would soon get over her jealous hatred of Psyche, but she hadn't, and now he decided to intervene.

Jupiter called the gods together and made a speech saying that he thought it was time that Cupid was married. It so happened, Jupiter went on, that Cupid was in love with someone who was going to give birth to his child. Perhaps he should marry her? Did they agree? 'Why not?' they all said. And that would mean, Jupiter said, that she would be immortal. Did they agree? 'Plenty of room, why not?' they all said. Really, the gods weren't much bothered either way.

So, at a great celebration, first Psyche was handed a certificate proving that she had achieved immortality, then she and Cupid were officially, divinely married.

Venus didn't know whether to be cross or to cry, and did a bit of both. Then, soon after the celebration, she became a grandmother, and didn't seem to mind a bit. In fact Venus recovered so much of her beauty that people began to stop her in the street again to say how gorgeous she was. Perhaps it was because she had a new interest in life, her beautiful grandchild.

34

Aeneas and Dido

When the Greeks burnt down Troy, there were only a few survivors. A Roman writer, Virgil, in his famous book *The Aeneid*, tells the story of how a small group of them, led by Aeneas, a Trojan prince, built a handful of ships and set sail to find a new home. They wandered west across the Mediterranean, meeting adventures and disasters, and after many years landed in Italy. One of these adventures took them, against their will, to Africa. They were sailing up the western coast of Sicily, aiming at last for Italy, when a huge storm blew up and drove them back south all the way to Africa. The storm had been created by Juno, an enemy of Aeneas. The Trojans landed near Carthage, and were taken to the court of the Queen of Carthage, Dido, where they received a warm welcome. She herself had been driven from her home in Tyre, and sympathized with their plight.

It was after midnight. For the first time in many months, Aeneas, resting on a couch amongst deep cushions, drinking from a heavy gold cup studded with gems, felt free of trouble. Dido thought how splendid he looked.

That same afternoon, entering the brand-new palace, the Trojans had felt out of place. They had stared in amazement at the weighty gold lamps hanging from the ceiling, the rich coverings on the couches, the gleaming thread of new tapestries. Even the wood of the tables looked freshly cut and stained.

Those few hours ago, in the polished marble of the walls and floors, the Trojans first saw their own dirty and exhausted reflections. Now, bathed and newly clothed, they could look at themselves with pleasure, and enjoy the sight of torches, jewellery and servants carrying food.

To welcome the refugees from Troy, Dido had decided to give a feast, one of the first in her new city of Carthage. For an afternoon and an evening all work stopped on the nearly finished harbour and the new main street, and the workers prepared the palace instead.

Now, after midnight, everyone had finished eating. Earlier that day, Aeneas had already told Dido about his escape from Troy, and how he had carried his father, Anchises, through the burning city. Now Dido was anxious to hear more.

'Aeneas, are you willing to tell us about your wanderings since the burning of Troy, and how you came here?'

'I am willing, Dido. I will tell you what has happened to us since we left Troy's shores for the last time, knowing we would never see our home again.'

Aeneas placed his cup on the table. Gazing out to the moonlit harbour and the glimmering sea beyond, as if he were staring back into the past, he began.

'We spent weeks building a few small ships, from timber growing by the shore, using tools we saved from Troy. Finally came the fateful morning when we found ourselves sailing away, leaving home. I looked back at the mountains, the empty harbour, the charred jetties, and the plain where Troy had been. There was no city, only a few shapeless mounds and ruins on the flat plain, fragments of wall, the rubble of houses.

'It was hard to leave, but better to start afresh, to rebuild the luck of the Trojan people somewhere far from Troy. We had no sign yet from god or priest about where to go. It was for me as leader to decide, or perhaps for the winds to decide for me. Nudged along by faithful breezes that seemed to know where they were taking us, we sailed to the island of Delos. There we asked the priest of Apollo where our destined home was. He said, "Return to the land of your ancestors."

'My blind father said to me, "The priest must mean Crete, where our ancestor Teucer was born." Others had heard of abandoned lands in Crete, left by Greeks who never returned from Troy. Crete it must be, we thought.

'We put to sea, and at sunrise on the third day we beached our boats on the yellow sands of Crete. There was plenty of rich land, which the Cretan Greeks had left behind when they went to Troy. I allotted farms and made laws. We sowed the fields, we started to build a city.

'But no rain fell to bless our new fields, the new crops withered, many died. One night, when the moon was full, I slept badly. I saw in a dream the small bronze figures I had carried out of Troy, our home-gods. They were gazing at me, speaking to me: "Apollo makes us say this. Italy he meant, not Crete. Italy, from where Dardanus came, the first ancestor."

'I told my father my dream. He thought for a while. "Italy, Italy . . . ah, yes," he said, "I remember. We Trojans had two groups of ancestors. One group were the sons and daughters of Teucer, who came from Crete, the other of Dardanus, who came from Italy. And now something else comes back to my mind. Cassandra, the prophetess, once told me that Italy – Hesperia she called it – was where we should go once Troy fell."

'So, off again, westwards this time. It had to be, though there were some who were so weary they decided to stay behind, to make a life for themselves in Crete if they could. Whether they succeeded I do not know.

'After a few hours we were out of sight of any land. Then Juno succeeded in persuading Neptune to raise a storm against us. Suddenly, out of a blue sky rose a thunderhead like a black cliff. There was nowhere to dash for shelter. The water went grey, a wind whitened the wave-tops. In a few minutes we were diving into dark troughs, then being tipped dizzily backwards as the boat climbed to the crest. We floundered there with a moment's view of the other boats before we slid shaking down to the trough again.

The Harpies

'Somehow we survived this terror, then there were three days and nights of calms and fog. Palinurus, our steersman and navigator, could not find a single star. At sunrise on the fourth day we saw a group of islands. We headed for them. Thanking Jupiter, Apollo, home-gods, everyone we could think of, we landed. The first thing we saw was a flock of goats wandering without an owner. A feast! A windfall!

'We did not know, as we slaughtered the animals and prepared our feast by the sea's edge, that the islands were the home of the Harpies, foul-smelling creatures with the bodies of vultures and the faces of women, who perch in trees and on clifftops like twelve-foot cormorants. The goats were theirs.

'We heard shrieks and a clatter of wings, out at sea, then out of the glare of the sinking sun, low over the water, came the predatory Harpies, their long black bodies trailing shadows over the waves.

'Within a few seconds they were swooping over our tables, trailing a splashy bombardment of stinking excrement along the food. Then they flapped down, squawking and waddling over the piled meat, snatching up lumps in their claws. None of us will ever forget the sight and stench and sound of them, packed screaming on the tables, hacking at the food with their savage jaws.

'Some of the men drew swords, but they fanned empty air. The Harpies flapped round us unharmed, the cacophony of their cries deafening us. Then, as suddenly as they had come, they flew off and settled on the cliffs, preening and clucking.

'A huge, creaking "craw" came from the cliff. It was their leader, speaking a threatening prophecy out of its human face. "You will find your Italy, but not till famine finds you first, not till your teeth gnaw the tables in front of you, that carry no food."

38

Cyclops

'Next morning we put to sea again, and soon the island of the Harpies lay far astern. I had begun to wonder if we would ever reach our destination. We had landed here, then there, then somewhere else, sucked and swilled about by winds and waters, like a straw in a trough when pigs drink.

'And we were menaced once more before we reached this city of Carthage. It was our last adventure before we came here, but the most frightening.

'We sailed northwards, then turned across towards Italy. Along the shore of Sicily we went, and came to a beautiful rocky inlet, a natural harbour at the foot of the mighty, smoking mountain of Etna. We soon realized it was a dangerous place to stop. That day the forges of Vulcan were at work inside the mountain, rumbling under our feet and throwing up from the highest summit bursting fountains of fire and a rain of sparkling boulders. From time to time the rocks splashed into the sea, and falling ash dimmed the sun.

'In the caves under Etna live Vulcan's labourers. They are the giant one-eyed Cyclopes who work in his smithies and sleep nearby in caves. We were keen not to meet them.

'Out of the woods came a filthy, bearded creature with torn clothes. He said he was one of Ulysses' men, and told us a wild story about Ulysses hiding under a sheep and poking out a Cyclops' eye with a burning branch. Whether it was true or not I couldn't tell, but it made us wary. When he said there were a hundred or more of these creatures rambling about near the coast, I decided we should leave.

'I was too late, though, because crashing down through the trees came a hundred-foot giant – a Cyclops. He didn't see us, as he scrunched across the stony beach fifty yards from us. Even at that distance we could hear his grunting breath. He moved uncertainly. He seemed to be feeling his way ahead with a great pine trunk, tapping round for rocks lying in his way. I realized he was blind! It was the Cyclops Ulysses had blinded!

'He waded out till the water was up to his shins, then knelt down and started to rinse at his face. What was he doing? Then I realized. The blinded Cyclops was rinsing out his empty eye socket.

'It gave us an opportunity, while he was busy, to push the boats out and row off. But we hurried. In their panic the men let the oars creak and splash. The Cyclops reared up, with a hand to his ear. After a moment he roared. It was like twenty bears snarling in your face. We rowed like madmen, amidst the din of even louder roaring, so that we thought Mount Etna was splitting right open.

'It was not Etna, but a herd of Cyclopes galloping down through the forest to the shore, splintering down trees in their headlong charge, picking up huge rocks and boulders and hurling them at us. We were two or three hundred yards from land by this time, but the rocks crashed into the water all around us, lifting us up and swirling us round.

'Somehow we kept on going forward, and as we got further out from land, the turbulence died down. The shouting became faint, and died away. We had escaped again.

'But only to be blown to these shores and arrive in Carthage. A few days after escaping the Cyclopes, I thought we were finally on our way to the new city. We were in calm waters off the west coast of Sicily, sailing under a sky of pure blue. Then, out of nowhere, another storm drove us back south here, to Africa.'

Dido had been captivated by Aeneas' story. She thanked him. She didn't know that Venus was intervening in her life, encouraging her to forget about the harbour that still had to be finished, the half-built wall, the towers with the tall cranes standing idly next to them. Dido was thinking not about her new city but about her new passion.

41

The tragedy of Dido

The next day Dido showed Aeneas round her city. He admired the wide streets, the fine buildings rising on every side. He was tempted by the thought of staying. Perhaps the refugees from Troy could join forces with the refugees from Tyre. Together they would make Carthage the strongest city in the world.

The same thought was in Dido's mind. She wanted Aeneas to think, 'What a fine place! What opportunities to help found a great city!' She wanted him to stay.

Aeneas did stay, at first for a week, then two weeks, then a month. He spent his time hunting, feasting, making love. Dido thought of herself as married to him. She no longer supervised the engineering works and the building. The towers of Carthage grew no higher. The cranes stood idle by the harbour wall.

Venus began to grow restless at Aeneas' long stay in Carthage. Jupiter, king of the gods, was also growing impatient. Aeneas was like one of his own boats, beached on the shores of Africa. His destiny was to sail for Italy, not live a life of ease as Dido's guest and lover.

Jupiter sent down Mercury, the messenger-god, to speak to Aeneas. Mercury found him giving advice to some workers on a building site next to the palace. Even there, he was dressed in a rich cloak, with his jewelled sword at his waist.

Mercury spoke to him. 'Is this why you left Troy? To dawdle with a woman? To lay a few stones for a Carthaginian temple? Remember who you are. Remember the future that waits for you. Make the fleet ready, and leave Carthage. Do not tell Dido. She will try to prevent you.'

After Mercury's visit, Aeneas was a changed man. He realized that Carthage could never be his city, could never be Trojan. It was Dido's city, and her inspiration. It belonged to her and her refugees from Tyre.

Dido knew something was wrong. Aeneas was preoccupied, and when a rumour came to her that the Trojan ships were being secretly repaired and made ready for sea, she realized the terrible truth.

She confronted Aeneas with his treachery. 'You were going to leave without telling me! You're married to me, in the sight of heaven, and I've risked everything for you. Yet now you calmly get ready to leave, and say nothing! Is that what I deserve? Why are you going? Or are you scared that some god will be cross with you for dawdling? Is that it?'

'Dido,' Aeneas replied, 'I would never have left without speaking. For me to stay here is impossible. This is your city, not mine. Another city waits for me, somewhere in the future. Every night my father's ghost comes to me and reminds me of it. Though we loved each other and said "husband" and "wife" to each other, we were never married. We only thought of ourselves as being married; we never went through the proper ceremonies. I cannot feel I leave you like a treacherous husband, only as an unreliable lover. Please understand.'

'I understand that you're going, and I understand that you're a coward and liar who has convenient dreams. Someday you'll understand what you have done.'

'I can't disobey. I'm not going of my own free will.'

Dido looked at him scornfully. 'You have no will of your own? Others make your mind up for you? And you say your mother was a goddess! The flint goddess of ingratitude, or more likely some misty goddess of weakness. You've shown me no pity, and now you can't even speak honestly.' She ran from him in tears.

Aeneas went back to his ships. The men brought the wood for their new oars out of hiding places in the forests. For days the beach was busy with the preparations of the Trojans.

Sick with dismay and longing, Dido could see them from her tower. She could only watch as the Trojan men swarmed over the ships, making the sails ready, bringing new timber from the woods to make repairs, scraping the hulls clean.

That night, Dido arranged for a huge pyre to be built in the palace yard. She said that she was going to burn all Aeneas' clothing, all his weapons, the tapestries from their bed. 'I want to be rid of everything that reminds me of him,' she told her maid. 'Including,' she added to herself, in her terrible grief, 'myself. My abandoned self.'

Next morning Dido could hardly bear to watch as the Trojan fleet rowed out of the harbour in the fresh dawn light, and the white sails, flapping, swung the ships north towards Sicily. She watched from her tower as they went slowly towards the horizon and finally disappeared. As soon as they were completely out of sight, Dido felt that her life was over.

In his boat Aeneas only once or twice turned his gaze north, towards Italy and the future. The rest of the time he looked behind him at diminishing Carthage and Dido, thinking constantly that there was still time to turn round. In a few hours he could be with Dido again.

As he gazed back, he saw a small column of smoke rising above the receding city. What could it be? It was a trap, he thought, a clever ruse to make him go back. The night before, Mercury had come in a dream to warn him that Dido might plot some last-minute deception against him. That decided it. They would sail on to Italy. Some other day, perhaps, he could return to Carthage.

But in Carthage the people were already bewailing the death of their Queen.

Notes

Aeneas (say I-nee'-us) (p. 5, 35-45)
A Trojan prince, the son of Venus and Anchises. He is the main character in *The Aeneid*, which tells how a group of Trojans escaped from Troy after it was burnt down, and settled in Italy as the first 'Romans'.

Apollo (p. 23, 36, 38)
One of the chief Roman – and Greek – gods. He had two famous temples, one at Delphi, where his priests made their prophecies, the other on the island of Delos.

Carthage (p. 13-14, 35-36, 41, 43-45)
A city in North Africa, near the modern Tunis.

Cerberus (say Sur'-bur-us) (p. 31)
King Pluto's watch-dog. He was a monster with many heads – in some stories as many as fifty.

Charon (say Kehr'-un) (p. 31)
The ferryman whose boat carried the dead over the River Styx.

Cupid (p. 5, 22-34)
A son of Venus, and a Roman god of love. In stories and paintings he is shown as a boy. He had a bow and arrows, which he shot into people's hearts to make them fall in love. His Greek name was Eros.

Cyclopes (say Sy'-clop-eez) (p. 40-41)
One-eyed giants. Many of them were supposed to live in Sicily, where they worked in Vulcan's forges. They made Jupiter's thunderbolts. Rumblings under the volcano of Etna meant the Cyclopes were at work.

Dido (say Die'-doh) (p. 35-45)
Queen of Carthage, the city she founded. She had fled to Africa from Tyre, in Phoenicia, after the death of her husband, and asked the king of Numidia for 'as much land as could be covered by an ox-hide'. When he agreed, she cut the skin into strips and surrounded enough land to begin a city.

Harpies (say Harp'-eez) (p. 38, 40)
Monsters with wings and women's faces. They were supposed to be able to snatch people up and carry them off. Sometimes they were described just as violent winds. They had names like 'Storm Wind' and 'Dark Flight'.

Juno (say Joo'-noh) (p. 30, 37)
The wife of Jupiter. She was believed to protect women in marriage and childbirth. The month of June, once called Junonius, was a favourite time for weddings. Juno's Greek name was Hera.

Jupiter (p. 34, 38, 43-44)
The king of the gods. He was married to Juno. His Greek name was Zeus.

Latin
The language of the Romans, of their books and everyday speech. Modern languages like Italian, Spanish and French have developed from the Latin spoken in those areas at the end of the Roman Empire.

Latium (p. 4, 6, 10-11)
The part of Italy in which Aeneas and the Trojans are supposed to have settled. The word 'Latin' is derived from 'Latium'.

Laugh Week (p. 17, 21)
The festival of the god Laughter.

Mercury (p. 44)
The messenger-god and the god of trade. He represented peace and prosperity. His Greek name was Hermes.

Neptune (p. 37)
God of the sea. His Greek name was Poseidon.

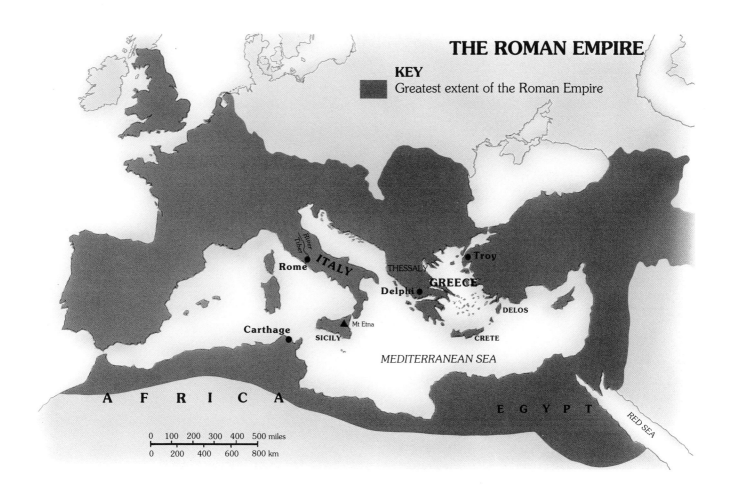

THE ROMAN EMPIRE

KEY
Greatest extent of the Roman Empire

Styx (say Stiks)   (p. 31)
A river in Tartarus, the underworld. Its waters were black. The souls of the dead had to cross the Styx to begin their afterlife in Tartarus. The ferryman Charon took them over, provided they could pay him one obol, a Roman and Greek coin.

Tartarus (say Tar'-tu-rus)   (p. 31)
The Roman – and Greek – underworld. It was ruled by Pluto and Proserpine, whose Greek names were Hades and Persephone.

Tiber (say Tie'-burr)   (p. 4, 6, 10-11)
The river on which Rome stands.

Venus   (p. 5, 18, 22-23, 29-31, 34, 41, 43)
Goddess of love. Julius Caesar claimed he was a descendant of hers (and of her son Aeneas) and dedicated a temple to her. Her Greek name was Aphrodite.

Virgil (say Vur'-jil) (p. 35)
A writer who lived from 70 to 19 BC. He was the author of *The Aeneid*, and perhaps the most well-known Roman writer of all, famous even in his own lifetime.

Vulcan (p. 40)
God of fire. His name gives us our English word 'volcano'. Volcanoes were supposed to be located above the forges of Vulcan.

Further Reading

Roman Myths and Legends, John Snelling
(Wayland, 1988)

The Roman World, Mike Corbishley
(Kingfisher Books, 1986)

Heroes, Gods and Emperors from Roman Mythology,
Henry Usher (Peter Lowe, 1983)

The All-colour Book of Roman Mythology,
Peter Croft (Octopus Books, 1974)

Imperial Rome, Sorrell, Alan and Anthony Birely
(Lutterworth, 1970)

The Eagle of the Ninth, Rosemary Sutcliffe
(Penguin, 1954)